A NOTE TO PARENTS

Reading Aloud with Your Child

Research shows that reading books aloud is the single most valuable support parents can provide in helping children learn to read.

- Be a ham! The more enthusiasm you display, the more your child will enjoy the book.
- Run your finger underneath the words as you read to signal that the print carries the story.
- Leave time for examining the illustrations more closely; encourage your child to find things in the pictures.
- Invite your youngster to join in whenever there's a repeated phrase in the text.
- Link up events in the book with similar events in your child's life.
- If your child asks a question, stop and answer it. The book can be a means to learning more about your child's thoughts.

Listening to Your Child Read Aloud

The support of your attention and praise is absolutely crucial to your child's continuing efforts to learn to read.

- If your child is learning to read and asks for a word, give it immediately so that the meaning of the story is not interrupted. DO NOT ask your child to sound out the word.
- On the other hand, if your child initiates the act of sounding out, don't intervene.
- If your child is reading along and makes what is called a miscue, listen for the sense of the miscue. If the word "road" is substituted for the word "street," for instance, no meaning is lost. Don't stop the reading for a correction.
- If the miscue makes no sense (for example, "horse" for "house"), ask your child to reread the sentence because you're not sure you understand what's just been read.
- Above all else, enjoy your child's growing command of print and make sure you give lots of praise. *You are your child's first teacher—and the most important one. Praise from you is critical for further risk-taking and learning.*

—Priscilla Lynch
Ph.D., New York University
Educational Consultant

To Jordan
—G.M.

To Taylor Duffy and Austin Geary,
in hopes that this book will comfort them
if and when they see their first spots.
—B.L.

LIBRARY OF CONGRESS CATALOGING-IN-PUBLICATION DATA

Maccarone, Grace.
    Itchy, itchy chicken pox / by Grace Maccarone; illustrated by Betsy Lewin.
        p.   cm. — (Hello reader)
    "Level 1."
    Summary: Peppy rhymes present the humorous side to a common ailment.
    ISBN 0-590-44948-6
    [1. Chicken pox—Fiction.   2. Stories in rhyme.]   I. Lewin, Betsy, ill.   II. Title.   III. Series.
PZ8.3.M127It   1992
[E]—dc20   91-16695
                                                                          CIP
                                                                          AC

        Text copyright © 1992 by Grace Maccarone.
        Illustrations copyright © 1992 by Betsy Lewin.
        All rights reserved. Published by Scholastic Inc.
    CARTWHEEL BOOKS is a trademark of Scholastic Inc.
    HELLO READER! is a registered trademark of Scholastic Inc.
24 23 22 21 20   4   5   6/9
                    Printed in the U.S.A.   09
            First Scholastic printing, May 1992

Itchy, Itchy Chicken Pox

by Grace Maccarone
Illustrated by Betsy Lewin

Hello Reader! — Level 1

Cartwheel
B·O·O·K·S ™

Scholastic Inc.
New York   Toronto   London   Auckland   Sydney

A spot.
A spot.
Another spot.

Uh-oh!
Chicken pox!

Under my shirt.
Under my socks.

Itchy, itchy
chicken pox.

Don't rub.
Don't scratch.

Oh, no!
Another batch!

On my tummy,
between my toes,

down my back, on my nose!

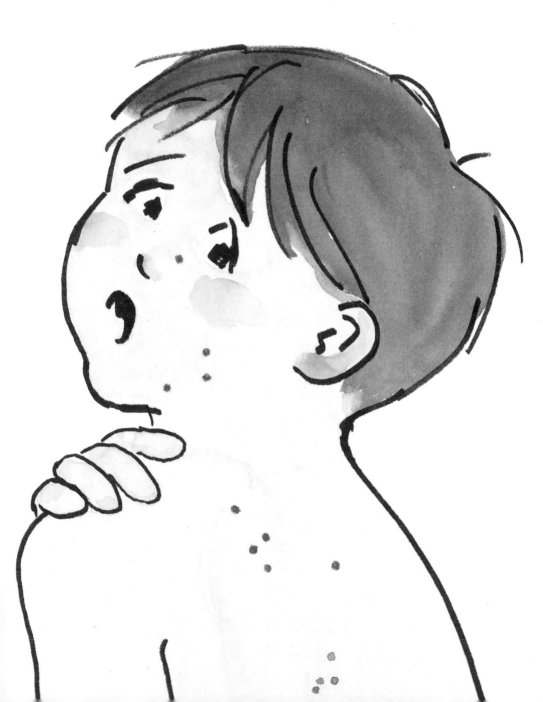

Lotion on.
Itching's gone
just for now.

It comes back—
OW!

One and two
and three and four.
Five and six...
and more and more.

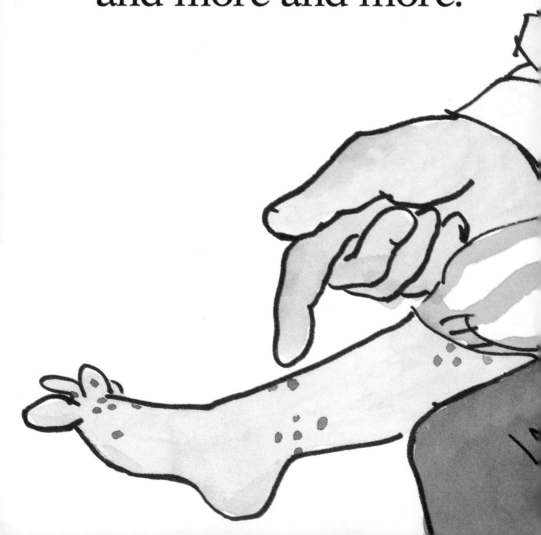

Daddy counts
my itchy spots.
Lots and lots
of chicken pox.

Itchy, itchy,
I feel twitchy....

I run away.
The itching stays.

Rubber ducky doesn't
like my yucky, mucky
oatmeal bath.
But Mommy says
it's good for me.

I rest.

I read.

I eat.

I play.

I feel better
every day.

And then…
no new spots.
Hooray!

I'm okay!
I get to go
to school today!